Truck Pals on the Job

Lawni Takes the Field

written and illustrated by Ken Bowser

RED CHAIR PRESS™

Funny Bone Readers and Funny Bone Books are published by Red Chair Press
Red Chair Press LLC   PO Box 333   South Egremont, MA 01258-0333
www.redchairpress.com

For my Grandson, Liam Hayden Bowser
who never met a truck he didn't like.

Publisher's Cataloging-In-Publication Data
Bowser, Ken.

   Lawni takes the field / written and illustrated by Ken Bowser.

     pages : illustrations ; cm. -- (Funny bone readers. Truck pals on the job)

   Summary: The field isn't ready for the big game. Will Lawni be ready to pitch in to
help the big machines complete the job?

   Interest age level: 004-008.

   ISBN: 978-1-63440-074-9 (library hardcover)

   ISBN: 978-1-63440-075-6 (paperback)

   Issued also as an ebook. (ISBN: 978-1-63440-076-3)

   1. Trucks--Juvenile fiction. 2. Athletic fields--Juvenile fiction. 3. Teams in the
workplace--Juvenile fiction. 4. Self-esteem--Juvenile fiction. 5. Friendship--Juvenile
fiction. 6. Trucks--Fiction. 7. Athletic fields--Fiction. 8. Teams in the workplace--Fiction.
9. Self-esteem--Fiction. 10. Friendship--Fiction. I. Title.

PZ7.B697 La 2016

[E]   2015938006

Printed in the United States of America
Distributed in the U.S. by Lerner Publisher Services. www.lernerbooks.com

1015 1P WRZSP16

It was a bright, sunny morning and
Lawni was excited to be back at
the ballpark. It was the last game
of the season and the biggest game
of the year!

Like every day, she watched quietly from the sidelines as Sali, the #1 mower began to prepare the field for the game.

"I'm just a backup mower. I'll never cut the grass on the big field," Lawni thought. She rode off to trim the small patch of grass outside the gate.

Lawni had studied Sali's work for years. Sali knew just how to prepare the grounds for the game. She cut the grass in perfect, straight lines.

She trimmed the edges with care
and made sure the field was level
and smooth. She knew just how to
make the field look extra nice.

Sali paid extra close attention to her work. Sometimes she would even crisscross the field to form a nice, diamond pattern in the grass.

Sali was a real artist. Watching
her work inspired Lawni to do her
very best work too. It also made
her feel kind of small.

Lawni would often daydream of a time
that she might be able to prepare the
big field all by herself. She would race
across the open grass!

Her motor purring as she made perfectly straight lines. She imagined the rest of the field crew cheering her on as she worked. "Go, Lawni!" they would cheer.

But Lawni knew that she was only the
backup mower. "I guess I should just
be happy trimming the patches outside
the gate," she thought.

Lawni could still dream and wish big
though! She got lost in her thoughts
again as she relaxed in the warm
afternoon sun.

Then a noise shook Lawni from her daydream! "SNAP!" "What was THAT?" she jumped. The loud noise had come from Sali's direction!

Lawni and Coach Turf raced to Sali's side. "My axel has worn out," said Sali. "Don't worry though. I'll be fine. It can be fixed. Just not today."

"Well, that's it," Coach Turf said.
"We will have to cancel the big game.
We can't play on a messy, half-cut field
like this. What a shame," he groaned.

16

Then Lawni had a great idea.
"I can finish the field, Coach!"
she shouted. "I've learned from Sali
and I've practiced every day!
PUT ME IN, COACH!"

Coach Turf thought for a while. He looked at the half-cut field. He looked at Lawni's confident face. "Okay, kid!" he boomed. "Let's see what you've got!"

18

"You won't be sorry, Coach!" beamed
Lawni. "I can do this! I KNOW I
CAN," she said. "You'll see!" she
roared as she raced onto the field!

Coach Turf and Sali watched from
the sidelines as Lawni went quickly to
work. Her lines were straight and true.
Here edges were square and sharp.

She made fast work of the grounds
and trimmed everything level and
smooth. When Lawni was finished
the field looked better than ever!

The entire field crew cheered. The big game was back on! "Great job, Lawni!" said Coach Turf. "I should never have doubted you, kid!"

From that day on Lawni and Sali worked side by side. "We are a team!" said Couch Turf. "From now on we all work together!" It was a great day at the ballpark.

Big Questions: Have you ever wanted to do something you were told you were not old enough or big enough to do? Is this how Lawni felt?

Big Words:

backup: someone or something that can be used as needed

inspired: gives a positive feeling, as a role-model